First published 2010 by
Mabecron Books
42 Drake Circus
Plymouth
PL4 8AB

Illustrations Rebecca Cobb
Designed by Peter Bennett

Typeset in Baskervlle2 BT
Printed in Italy

978-0-9532-15690

For Hugo

The Ferry Birds

HELEN DUNMORE

Illustrations by Rebecca Cobb

Mabecron Books

Jago and Mum crossed the water on the ferry to see Great-Gran. 'There's Great-Gran on the quay, waving her red handkerchief!' said Jago. Jago and Mum waved back.

The two turnstones on the ferry bow flapped their wings and flew off to a buoy.

'Those turnstones were ferry passengers, just like us,' said Jago.

'They make the journey every morning,' said Mum. 'When we go home, those two turnstones will go back on the ferry too.'

'How do you know?'

'Topper told me,' said Mum. Topper was the skipper of the ferry, and Mum had known him all her life.

Great-Gran's cottage was full of treasures. When she was young, Great-Gran was a pilot. She flew aeroplanes called Spitfires from the factory to the airfields. Great-Gran let Jago put on her flying jacket and her flying goggles.
'I wish I could fly,' said Jago.

Jago told Great-Gran about the two turnstones who travelled on the ferry.
'I wonder why they go back and forth every day.'
'That's their secret,' said Great-Gran. 'Maybe one day they'll tell you, Jago. You'd better make friends with those Ferry Birds quick, because they'll be flying off to the Far North once the warm weather comes.'

'The Far North!' said Jago, and his eyes sparkled. 'That's where Dad is!' Dad's work was in the Far North because he was exploring the rocks there for precious metals. Jago missed him very much. He wrote letters to Dad and sent him drawings. Mum made a chart which showed how many days it was until Dad came home. Every bedtime they crossed off one more day.

'Maybe those Ferry Birds know Dad,' Jago said to Great-Gran.

'Maybe they do,' she agreed.

One day Mum hurt her leg. She had to rest, but Jago longed to go on the ferry to see the Ferry Birds and Great-Gran. 'You can go if you're sensible,' said Mum. 'I'll ask Topper to keep an eye on you, and Great-Gran will meet you at the quay.'

Topper told Jago to sit near the Ferry Birds.
  'Maybe they'll tell you their secrets,' said Topper.
Jago moved up until he was right by the Ferry Birds.
They looked as if they wanted to talk to him.
'I'm good at keeping secrets,' said Jago.
The Ferry Birds looked all around to be sure no one else could hear.
'Do you know my Dad in the Far North?' asked Jago.
They bobbed their heads.
'I promise I won't tell anyone,' said Jago.

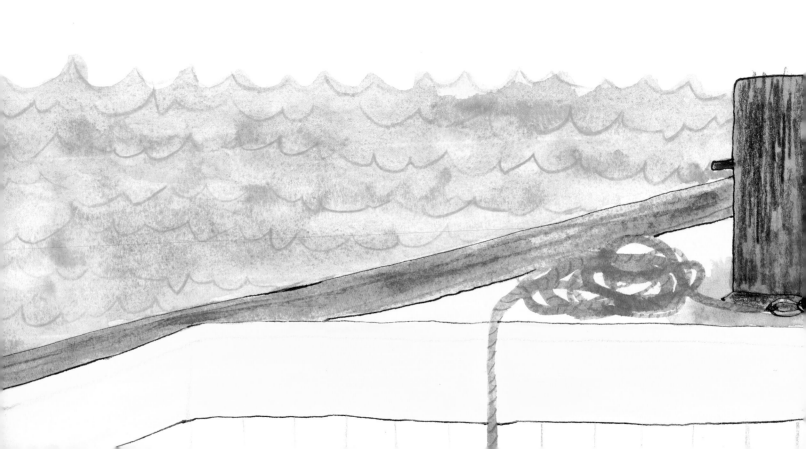

'The Ferry Birds' voices were small and only Jago heard them.
'What does your father look like?' they asked.
'He's tall and he has red hair and when he comes home he opens his arms like this and gives me the biggest hug in the world.'
The birds bobbed their heads again.
'We will ask the Pilot,' they said.
'Who is the Pilot? Is he a pilot like my Great-Gran?'
'The Pilot is the leader of all the turnstones,' said the Ferry Birds mysteriously.

'Why do you go back and forth on this ferry every day?' asked Jago.
The Ferry Birds looked at each other.

'We have work to do on the other shore,' said one.

'We pick up feathers which fall from flying birds.'

'We pick up fine pieces of seaweed.'

'And then the Pilot calls all the turnstones to weave them into a blanket of seaweed.'

'And a quilt of feathers and spider-silk.'

'For any traveller we meet in the South Country who wants to fly with us to the Far North.'

'Is this the South Country?' asked Jago.

'Of course,' said the Ferry Birds.

'Am I the traveller who wants to fly to the Far North?' asked Jago.

'We think so. But first you'll have to ask the Pilot.'

Great-Gran was delighted that Jago had come to visit her all on his own.

'You're a proper traveller now, Jago,' she said. Jago put on Great-Gran's flying jacket and flying goggles.

Great-Gran said, 'You can take those home with you, Jago. You're old enough to keep them now. Mind you show them to the Ferry Birds.'

That night, Jago went to sleep with the flying jacket and flying goggles beside his bed. In the middle of the night he woke up. He heard a tapping sound on his bedroom window. The moon was high and outside he saw his friends the Ferry Birds. There was a bigger turnstone with them, and Jago guessed it was the Pilot. He opened his window.

'Does your father have hair as red as a forest fire?' asked the Pilot.
'Yes!'
'Does your father whistle like a bird when he's working?'
'Yes!'
'Is your father tall and laughing?'
'YES!'
'Then I've seen him in the Far North,' said the Pilot. 'We turnstones
know where he is.'
'Can you take me to him?' asked Jago.
'Yes, if you're brave enough,' said the Pilot.
How will you take me?' asked Jago.
'You'll see,' said the Pilot.

'All the turnstones are coming. Get ready.'
Jago put on his Great-Gran's flying jacket and goggles and his
own stout boots. He climbed out of the window and ran into the
middle of the grass that sloped away from his house. He looked up at
the night sky where the moon shone.
Suddenly the sky was filled with turnstones. They swooped, holding
a blanket of woven seaweed in their beaks. They hovered above the
grass, beating hard with their wings and holding out the blanket.

'Jump on!' said the Pilot, and he seized the leading corner of the blanket with his beak.
Jago jumped on. Hundreds of turnstone wings beat hard, and slowly the blanket began to lift. It tilted down the slope, accelerating and gaining flying speed ...   Jago was flying.

Jago peeped over the edge of the blanket. There was the roof of his house. There was his town and the lights along the dark harbour water. The blanket was lifting, lifting ...

The turnstones flew over the cliffs and over the wild ocean. They flew over ships and lighthouses and islands while the wind whistled past Jago's ears and the stars and moon shone brightly. At last Jago grew tired and he snuggled under his quilt and fell asleep to the sound of the turnstones' wings.

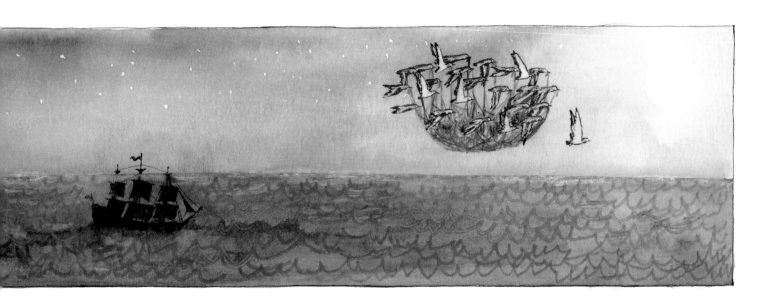

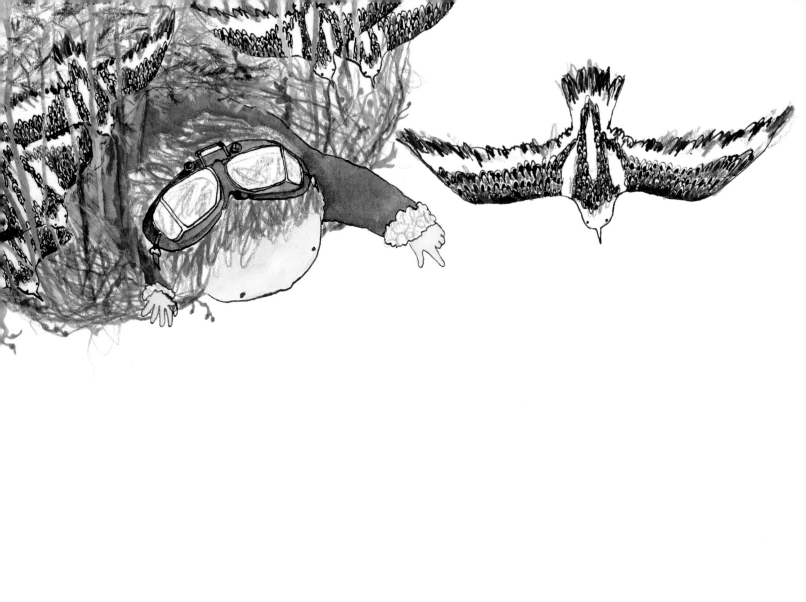

When he woke there was land below and it was getting light. The turnstones flew lower and lower. Jago saw forests and rocks and snow. It was very cold and he was glad he was wearing his flying jacket.

'Is this the Far North?' he wondered. He peered down and saw huts with smoke rising from them. He saw a man with red hair walking across the snow into a hut.

'Dad!' shouted Jago.

The turnstones circled down and down, with the Pilot flying ahead. 'Prepare for landing!' called the Pilot.

The turnstones landed in a secret place behind the huts. Jago jumped from the blanket onto the snow.

'We'll come back for you,' said his friends the Ferry Birds. 'Listen for our wings, Jago.'

Jago waved to the turnstones as the blanket rose into the air. He dodged past the huts and scooted around a snowmobile. There was a set of footprints in the snow. Jago followed them to the door of a hut, and then he turned the handle and went in.

Dad was reading a letter from Jago. He looked up in amazement and then opened his arms wide as Jago ran to him. Dad lifted Jago high above his head and then gave him the biggest hug in the world.

Dad took Jago to the canteen and ordered a pile of pancakes dripping with maple syrup.
All Dad's friends asked, 'Whose boy is this?'
Dad said proudly, 'This is my boy, Jago.'

Dad took Jago for a ride on his snowmobile across the snowy tundra. They heard wolves howling, but the wolves didn't come close. Jago was safe with Dad and he was warm in his flying jacket. He wished the journey would never end, but soon they were roaring back to camp.

Dad gave Jago a piece of quartz with gold veins in it.
'Keep it safe,' he said.
'I'll keep it safe for ever,' Jago promised. Just then he heard a distant beating of wings, and he knew that the turnstones were coming to take him home.
'I must go now, Dad,' said Jago.
Dad put his arms around Jago and they hugged each other for a long time.
'I'll be home soon,' said Dad.

Jago slipped away behind the huts. A moment later the turnstones swooped down with the blanket.

'Jump on!' called the Pilot. Jago scrambled onto the blanket.

'Prepare for take-off!' The turnstones beat their wings and rose higher and higher, with the blanket held tight in their beaks.

Jago peeped over the edge of the blanket and saw the camp far below him. Soon they were flying away from the Far North. Jago was full of pancakes and he was tired from travelling. He fell asleep, curled under his quilt.

Just as the moon set, the turnstones brought Jago home.
  'Goodbye, goodbye! Thank you for taking me to the Far North to see
my father!'
'Goodbye, Jago.' Jago waved and waved as the turnstones soared into
the sky.

The next day Jago went to see Great-Gran. Some passengers were talking about the Ferry Birds.
'I wonder why they go back and forth every day?'
'Nobody knows.'
'We know, don't we?' whispered Jago to his friends.

Great-Gran waved her red handkerchief from the quay as the ferry came in. The Ferry Birds flew to their buoy, and Jago climbed the steps and showed Great-Gran his piece of quartz with the veins of gold in it.

'I think that comes from a far country,' said Great-Gran.

'It comes from a very far country,' said Jago, 'But it's a secret, Great-Gran. Maybe one day the Ferry Birds will tell you.'